MELODIES OF TRANSFORMATION: A K-POP JOURNEY

UNVEILING LIANNA'S WORLD OF MUSIC, FRIENDSHIP, AND SELF-DISCOVERY

ROMA VUDUTALAPALLY

Contents

Acknowledgements

I want to express my gratitude to many people who played a crucial role in getting this novel published. First and foremost, I owe a huge thank you to my teacher, Akrsti Aggarwal. She not only guided me through the publishing process but also provided unwavering support throughout my writing journey. I'm truly grateful.

I also want to extend my heartfelt thanks to my parents, Srividya Boinapalli and Naveen Vudutalapally. Their endless support and valuable feedback have been instrumental in shaping this novel into what it is today.

Additionally, I am indebted to a number of friends whose ideas and inspiration have fueled my creativity along the way. Your contributions have truly made a difference. Thank you all.

Fans from around the world have been attracted to a new, popular sensation called K-pop or Korean pop. K-pop groups are full of young women and men who create amazing choreographies and catchy songs they have produced. Recently, the song genre has become very popular; it's been found in numerous popular places to listen to songs, such as Spotify and Apple Music. Even YouTube has added K-pop as a genre to its music page.

There is now an increased demand for plastic surgery because people obsess over their looks. Oli London spent nearly thousands of dollars to look like BTS's Jimin and a BLINK (a fan of Blackpink) spent millions of dollars to look like BLACKPINK's Lisa. People who look at them and wish to be like them or to be them because of their money and happiness but are fooled. Yet they seem happy with who they are with and what they do.

Sometimes, it's just a mask for how empty they feel inside. Singers and bands receive hate; this may seem petty, but the reasons people hate are also petty. For example, as a soloist K-pop singer and actor, IU is hated for being BTS's Jungkook's ideal type. This is an example of a very petty reason to hate! Hate may not seem like a big problem, but it can lead to something big.

Hate for many K-pop idols leads to depression, and that depression can devour them and lead them to take their life. SHINee member Jonghyun took his life; he talked about wanting to run from his pain and told of the pressure of being in the spotlight for nearly a decade. The main sentence in the note read, "I am broken from the inside. The depression that has slowly eaten me away has finally consumed me, and I couldn't beat it." It's been about 4 years since we lost this angel. I know he's looking down on SHINee, standing on the stage and singing with them. The K-pop industry is full of happy and depressing memories. It hurts to know what your idols do daily to make their families and fans happy. The battles they face along the way are insane. No one realizes how much pain idols go through; your idol could feel like killing themselves, but you would never know. Idols deserve the world, not just to be bashed, canceled, hurt, mistreated and rumored about.

Jonghyun was a soldier who lost the battle through depression, but we shouldn't think of his death; we should think about his talent and memories with SHINee and in the K-pop community. He was strong, generous, and a great main vocalist in SHINee. He stood proud on stage to hide all his emotions, to show he was 'okay' on the outside; on the inside, he was broken. We haven't lost a member of SHINee; one just gained his wings earlier.

If you're in the K-pop community to bash other idols, this could be them one day. Everyone is crying around them; please think before doing stuff. Every idol has feelings; they may have made a mistake, but we're humans. Idols were not born to be a punching bag. The K-pop community has gotten more toxic these days. People don't realize that you're breaking people's idols into pieces. Even if they've done something mistreating, racist, homophobic, etc. That isn't a reason to tell them to die;

not every idol knows what wrong thing they did. You can hold them accountable; of course, you can. But if you're not the one getting offended by it, then you have no involvement in that situation. A lot of whites speak over Blacks, Asians, Muslims, etc., but most of the time, it's not the whites getting hurt.

This is an example of SHINee-Jonghyun; like this, there are many more examples.

Another soloist, Goo Hara, has the same story: she died at the age of twenty-eight. Goo Hara was found dead at her home in November, and she is widely believed to have taken her own life after being targeted by abusive online comments. This may seem exactly the same as Jonghyun, but now we are asking, did Goo Hara RIP? You see, Goo Hara was left by her biological mother, who fought for the right to her inheritance even though it seems that she decided to leave Hara. At Hara's funeral, instead of mourning, she happily took pictures with other K-pop idols. Then, Hara's safe was stolen in January 2020, which is after her death, but what makes it more interesting is that it was believed that this person was close to Hara. Why? Well, the mystery person knew exactly where everything was, like the safe and where it was hidden; they also knew several other things about the house except for the security camera. People believe that it was either Hara's Biological mom or someone else who knew her very well. Were we really wishing her Rest In Peace?

Goo Hara's friend Sulli also committed suicide before Hara; she hung herself because of depression and cyberbullying. A few days ago, in her life, she acted happy, so no one ever knew that she was going to do the unexpected. In her life, she asked, "Why are you saying bad things about me? Why do I deserve this?" She later on said, "I am not a bad person; I'm sorry."

These are some of the saddest deaths in K-pop. Most people say K-pop songs are upbeat and about all sorts of happiness and love, but that's not true. Some BTS songs include songs that are about awareness purposes, such as racism. So, what is calling out to people struggling with the difficulties of everyday life? BTS gives a rousing shout of "So What" and tells people to follow their dreams without fear. In "Blue & Grey", BTS deals with the blues of being isolated and feeling abandoned. The song talks about people's struggles with depression and how the once cheerful person they knew had become unrecognizable. All the colors from their lives have faded into "Blue & Grey". There are more songs about the awareness of racism, depression, bullying, etc. Not all bands write about love and happiness; they also try to raise awareness about hate. K-pop idols also give speeches about awareness; they just don't do it to get a good name; they do this because they believe in what's right. Some people decide that they only do this to get a good name, but there is more than that; these people have also felt the wrath of racism and want to stop it. They feel that they do not want other young people to be targeted by this potential hate that helps depression along. We shouldn't just think of them as attention seekers or other things; We should also see them as activists.

Not only that, but many K-pop idols receive death threats. I can't imagine how frightened they are, but they always act like they never got a death threat. Some threats are the reason for possible suicide.

1
Early Life

Hwang Chae Yeong, at an early age, became amazed by people on TV, their acting, and the songs they published. She became interested in pursuing a career in the entertainment industry. She began to attend acting classes, but soon after 3rd grade, her family's financial situation took a path for the worst. Her parents moved to Daegu, Seoul City. She and her younger brother lived far apart from their parents; they moved to Gangnam, Seoul City, with their grandmother. Chae Yeong barely had contact with her parents but felt safe in her grandmother's care.

Chae Yeong was an excellent student, topping everyone she could. She continued acting classes and took some vocal classes, too. Chase Yeong was bullied a lot, but she didn't let anything take her down. She hoped that she would be a singer or actor. During middle school, Chae Yeong found her passion in singing after being applauded and cheered in a school play. She attended twenty-three auditions but failed all of them; she was also scammed by fake entertainment companies. She later tried to audition for any acting careers, but none of them would accept. At one audition, the company did not like her acting as much as her voice. This entertainment was called FIU Entertainment. She later trained at FIU Entertainment with many other friends. After signing with FIU Entertainment, Chae Yeong stated she loved living with her grandma and wouldn't move anywhere away from the family she had. FIU accepted this easily and let her stay in Gangnam, Seoul. Though she has an average job as a singer, her career caused a decrease in attending school and declining grades, with the exception of Korean literature. After graduating high school in 2012, she decided not to continue any more education, such as college and started with her singing career.

2
Career Beginnings

After training for ten months, Chae Yeong made her debut in 2008 under her stage name, conceived by FIU to mean "I and You become one through music." She performed her debut single, "Lost Child," live for the first time on the music program on September 18, 2008, making it her debut performance as a professional singer.

"Lost Child" is the lead single from her debut extended play "Lost and Found", which was released on September 24, 2008. For the album, Chae Yeong was awarded many awards in November of that same year. However, the album did not do well commercially. During an interview in 2011, Chae Yeong said, "My first album failed, but I'm grateful for that. If I had become successful as soon as I made my debut, I wouldn't appreciate my staff members and the popularity that I'm enjoying now."

On April 23, 2009, Chae Yeong launched her first studio album, *Growin' Up*, with the lead promotional single, "Later." She began her album promotion the next day, performing "Later" on LA32 Music Bank. The song was noted for its stark contrast in musical style to "Lost

Child," which was described as "heavy" and "dark" compared to the 1980s "retro sound" of "Later." The dance choreography, stage costume, and hairstyle shown in live performances were used to emphasize her youthfulness and project a "cute" image. Although it drew a favorable response from the public, Chae Yeong, who was fifteen years old at the time, admitted that the image made her feel awkward.

Several songs from Lost and Found were featured on her debut studio album *Growin' Up*, including "Do we Know?" A new rock-style arrangement of the song was released as the follow-up single to "Later." Toward the end of 2009, Chae Yeong released her second extended play, IN. She began promoting its lead single, "Marshmallow," on music programmes on November 13, 2009. Recalling the performances, Chae Yeong stated on a 2013 episode of *Happy Ever After* that she disliked having to wear the girlish costumes and hairstyle fashioned for the song promotions. The performances were well-received and were once again labeled "cute," reminiscent of reviews for "Later."

As her popularity began to rise, Chae Yeong made more frequent appearances on variety shows, performing on Star Silver Bell. Her acoustic covers of other artists' songs, such as Girls' "Gee," etc., featured in these live performances gained tremendous interest online. In late 2009, she became a television presenter for the first time, hosting a weekly music chart show on GomTV, while appearing as a fixed guest on multiple radio programmes such as Kiss, Money, Radio, etc.

3
Rising Popularity and Acting Debut

On June 3rd, 2010, Chae Yeong released "Forever With You". She performed this song in her world tour, and when she came back, she starred in a Korean movie, *Outerside*. The theme song was her newest song, "Break Through", a collaboration with a big star singer, Lee Yeon U. Chae Yeong also released a song while acting in her K-drama; she called this one "Whisper". Many people were surprised that in 2 months, 3-4 new songs were released. Since she composed, wrote, and sang all her songs, people called her very talented. She gained popularity fast since lots of songs came out quickly.

After starring in *Outerside* and gaining more respect and popularity, she decided to do another movie. She starred in a movie called *Fake and Real*. This was a major hit in her industry. She got lots of respect but also received multiple death threats and hate comments. After receiving one hate comment that stood out, she was motivated to turn it into a song; she called this song "Bad Dreams". In an interview, they mentioned "Bad Dreams".

They asked where the idea came from; Chae Yeong said that she made this song because she could have taken this in a bad way; instead, she wanted it to be different. She said that it was living a life you can't wake up from. She also mentioned that these hate comments could be a catchy song. Many K-pop idols were astonished by her answer and thought of this surprising idea. This became something popular, and Chae Yeong became more and more popular every day.

After "Bad Dreams", she made a song called "Voice". This song included many high-pitched tunes in the climax. After hearing how beautiful her voice is, she was praised for her vocal abilities. "Bad Dreams" and "Voice" were voted in 100 Greatest K-pop Songs. Since she was very popular at this time, she was on many interviews and shows; this was a great opportunity for her and the interviewers. She also went on two more shows as well. She filmed and sang at the same time, which meant a decrease in her rest time. She would only be able to get 2-3 hours of sleep a day. By the end of 2011, she had been able to complete 112 songs in total, but she was determined and did not give up.

She attended many interviews and comedy shows. She did get hate, racism; they would also shame her. She also got awarded with different prizes. Her annual salary increased greatly over the 2 years. She said her music would suit any age. She would often get requests about concerts, and that's when she decided to do it. She held many concerts, and she made new songs that had the highest number of views, such as "Cherry". She also held a friendship meet and greet with her fans. She received multiple Seoul awards; she was awarded the Best Singer of 2011 later in the fall.

In her album, eight out of eleven of her songs were chosen for one of her concerts. This was the longest concert she had ever performed; it was 4 hours long with 10-20 minute breaks from time to time. Chae Yeong also got asked what her stage name is. For a while, Chae Yeong thought about what the perfect stage name would be for her, and she chose Se Ri. Se Ri had gone through a lot of bad and good, but one thing was her manager. Her manager treated her poorly and sometimes hit her. When multiple clips of this were shown, he was thrown out. Se Ri has mentioned it was one of her happiest moments. When I see other idols, some have stage names so it is easier to call them than by their full name. I love Song See-ah's stage name; her stage name is Ari. Ari is a great singer.

4
Diary Entry 1

Dear Diary, March 18, 2011

I used to be interested in music that is upbeat, slow, and energetic. They used lots of English phrases, too, but I am into K-pop now. It all started one day when a 12-year-old girl with brown hair and blue eyes— that's me! I have a half-American and half-Korean look. My mom is from Korea, and my dad is from California. I have an English name and a Korean name. My Korean name is Lee Jae Yeon, and my English name is Lianna.

I never got into K-Dramas or K-pop, and my mom never forced me, but I did learn to love my culture. Every winter or summer (sometimes both), me and my family would travel there. I have an older brother and a twin brother, and they dislike their Korean names and prefer not to use them. We have a 7-year age gap.

I love Korea. It has beautiful views and cool places to visit. To be honest, I prefer Korea over America. I mean, it had so much cool and advanced technology that we didn't have in the US. People at school like me, and I have lots of friends. I know that there is potential racism against me, but I never really thought anything about it. No one has ever shown it to me or any of my family.

I started to like K-pop when my mom played a song by a soloist called Chae Yeong. Her vocals were great, and my mom introduced me to K-pop. Chae Yeong was really pretty, in my opinion. Her hair was naturally black and straight, but she dyed it other natural colors and sometimes curled or cut it. Chae Yeong barely applies makeup. She finds that using a toner helps keep her skin even, and she doesn't need to wear foundation or anything. She notes that she only puts a red dash on the bottom of her eyelid. She says it pops out more. She wears thin eyeliner and barely any mascara. She suggests using a lash formula that makes your eyelashes strong and healthy.

My mom didn't let me wear makeup. I used toner for a while before I was able to use makeup. I tried all of her hacks, and I looked stunning. Chae Yeong taught me so many things, like keeping a consistent routine from morning to night. Her music helps me calm down. I think I have found my enlightenment idol. Since I like Chae Yeong so much and she was part of the K-pop community, I decided to get to know more K-pop idols. I soon memorized almost thirty bands, including all the members' names. I found myself a huge fan of K-pop a couple of months after hearing Chae Yeong. Chae Yeong's dance style and her ability to compose songs quickly are two of my favorite things. I sometimes felt like Chae Yeong was overworking herself. Nevertheless, I didn't want to be rude in any way. Chae Yeong has some of the most outstanding songs in the whole K-pop community. I love all of her songs, but in my opinion, "Cherry" was overrated. I also felt like one of her other songs, "Accused," is pretty underrated. When I see other idols, some have stage names so it is easier to call them by their full name. I love Song See-ah's stage name; her stage name is Ari.

Ari has gorgeous hair, and she seems pretty likable. There has been a rumor about her apparently abusing her staff. I don't know what to believe until I see proof, so I am gonna stick with what I know.

5
Diary Entry 2

Dear Diary, March 19, 2011

It's been a very long time since I have liked K-pop, and no one at school knows. I think it's better if people know what I like, and maybe I can find someone who is interested in K-pop too! It sounds like a great idea. My teachers and classmates have been kind to me. I was helpful and smart in many ways. I have a very close friend, Maeve. She came from Indonesia, and she reminded me of a big K-pop star, Katie.

Katie was also from Indonesia, and they had similar facial features but a whole different personality. On camera, she was loud around everyone, even strangers. She hated studying and quiet places, while Maeve loved quiet places and loved studying. She was very quiet around people she didn't know, but since we were friends for a couple of years, I have seen her loud personality.

Our school may seem to be a trampoline with happiness bouncing from person to person, but it's not. There is one specific girl, Sue. She was supposedly "teasing" people, and she never got in trouble. She had never come to me before and talked to me, and she probably didn't know I existed, and I am VERY thankful for that. At home, everything is the best. It's peaceful and quiet, and my mom gives me the agency to ask for help when I need it and to do my own things. My family is perfect to me. School is almost over, and I find myself going to start a new grade. I decided to show my love for the K-pop industry in 7th grade. I don't like to be writing during the summer, so you won't see me for a couple of months, diary! Bye!

6
Diary Entry 3

Dear Diary, Aug 25, 2011

My whole family seemed to support me in liking K-pop, even my brothers, but I don't get why Maeve seemed reluctant to be ecstatic. She seemed confused and trying to act happy, but it didn't look like it. My mom said she was getting used to me going to a whole new stage. I said okay, and we continued to keep in contact. When school started, I decided not to run up to her and hug her because of how distant she was the other day, but surprisingly, SHE came up and hugged me. I started 6th grade. I had nine teachers and was excited. Our school was the best; we had a pool, a BIG one. It had five hidden hallways, and I loved it so much! My first class: Spanish! I was placed right next to Maeve! I had most of my classes together. I didn't talk about K-pop too much, but I hoped to find someone with interests similar to mine. We started with an introduction. I know it is so boring. I also had most classes with a boy named Xander. In Spanish, I was asked to give my name and a fact about myself. I couldn't think about anything except me liking K-pop. So when it was my turn, I stood up and said, "Hi, my name is Lianna, and I like K-pop." I sat back down, and everyone was silent. Very awkward. My next period was with Maeve again, and I was so happy we had a 10-minute passing period since the school was so big. Our art class was also in another hidden hallway, so while walking with Maeve, she asked me, "What songs do you think I should listen to?" I was taken aback but snapped back into reality. At that moment, I wanted to give her a list of songs, but I didn't. "You should listen to Accused," I blurted out. "Oh, okay, cool," was all she replied. We arrived at the art room 7 minutes before the bell rang. We came in and took seats next to each other. "Woah, this place is huge!" was what Maeve said when she walked in. "I know, right, Mimi!" (Mimi is my nickname for Maeve.) She asked me how long the song was, and I replied that it was 2-3 minutes. She said, "Okay, well, we got 5 minutes, let's listen." I was astonished. "Okay," was what I murmured. I opened my computer. After 3 minutes had passed, she said, "Oh, wow, that's good." "Yeah," is what I came up with since, 2 minutes in, we started talking about our classes.

The teacher walks in and says, "Let's talk about classroom rules, share our names, and I will pass out a paper for you and your parents to sign." We talked about how we should be kind and respectful, and apparently, we could eat in art with permission! I loved that we shared our names, and she passed out a signature paper about getting art supplies. This was due tomorrow; better not forget was the first thought in my head, and just like that, 42 minutes had passed. Ooh yay. "What's next period for you?" "World Cultures, you?" I replied. "No way!" she screamed, and we had the same period AGAIN. We got to our next period because it was on the whole other side of the school, not in a hidden hallway.

We walked in; the teacher assigned us to the same table. "Wow, our luck today," Maeve said with a wide smile. We had 2 minutes, so we pulled out our schedule, and now way! We had the exact same classes together at the right time and the right room number! "Yay!" we screamed. But oh no, someone had to ruin it. Sue smiled at us; she sat at the SAME table as us. "Noo," Maeve groaned in a whispering voice. "Hi, guys!" Sue looked at us, smiling ear to ear. Oh no, I thought. "Well, I am just gonna get in my seat, you know?" She laughed. Maeve passed me a note saying, "That's supposed to be funny?" I stifled my giggle. Maeve has a huge hatred toward her. We started with introductions; when it was my turn, I said, "Hi, my name is Lianna. I like K-pop, and I am best friends with Maeve." Mimi said, "Hi, my name is Maeve. I love to read, and I am Lianna's best friend." "Aww, matching," the teacher replied to our introduction. She then said it was Sue's turn, but what made me giggle a bit was that she said Sue's name as Suuee; Sue had to correct her two times. She said, "Hi, my name is Sue, and I am also best friends with Lianna." I turned to her, confused and mad. I spoke loud but not too loud, "I know we went to the same school and all, but we didn't even talk to each other, so why did you say that?" "Oh, sorry, you looked like one of my friends," she said. "I got carried away," she says, embarrassed. Maeve whispered in my ear. "That taught her, but what friends does she have?" We giggle together. The next period was advisory for me. I had Mrs. Loe, and so did Maeve. "This is clearly fate,"

#6

"Maeve said laughing." I laughed with her too. Sue caught up to us. Seeing us together, smiling and laughing, her face began to turn red. She walked right up to me and said, "Why did you embarrass me?"

"Wow, what was I supposed to say now?" I would say sorry I began, but you said you were my best friend when we haven't even known each other for 1 week. Like, what was I supposed to do? Then she just stormed off, speechless. Maeve was proud of me, but I knew I just caused trouble. It went on for about six more periods. Sue was in 3-4 classes with me in total! What a day.

Bye, Diary.

7
Entry 4

Dear Diary, August 31, 2011

I slowly fit in, but not as fast as I did in 5th grade. It was normal, right? Sue was already friends with probably the whole grade; anyone would take her side. Things got really, really fast. Maeve said she wouldn't be there for the first three classes. Bummer! So I had to face Sue alone. We had homework and lots of graded assignments. The next one was a big shock. Me, Maeve, Sue, Ava. This was a 2-week project worth a lot of our grade. The first day was without Maeve. Ava was Sue's new best friend. We had to work on something that shows creativity and talk about something interesting. We could make it in any style, for example, on a computer, on a poster board, etc. Ava started with a good idea of splitting what each of us was going to say. Ava is pretty nice, so it's really hard to know she's best friends with a devil. But soon, I realized she was half as bad. I proposed, "We can do an idea about a group and things we are interested in; we could talk about different species and cultures. I saw this idea on K-pop Vlive." Ava was silent, and they basically shouted, "K-pop, why are you always talking about K-pop, Lianna?"

I wanted to punch her so badly. This was tiring; Sue and Ava were off-topic the whole time. When Maeve came back in advisory, I told her all about it. We started our own research and got lots of work done. School went on for such a long time, and after school, I rushed home. I pushed through the crowded bus area. 1703 isn't here was my first thought, me and Maeve just talked during our waiting period. At one point, our bus came, and we went on and started talking about how different it was in elementary and middle school. I got off at my stop, and I almost jumped for joy. I, of course, finished my work and took a nice long nap; finally, the weekend! Things were going okay for me, but if I have to be honest, I know I didn't include this. However, after Sue announced, "Why are you so obsessed with comments?" people look at me differently. Tomorrow, my mom said that I can go shopping with Maeve. YAY.

Bye, diary.

8
Diary Entry 4

Dear Diary, Sept 1

It's finally a Saturday! I went shopping with Maeve, and it was really fun! I got 4 new shirts, two hoodies, some jewelry, some lotions, and perfumes, and they had the best food. We went to different stores like New Time Topic, where I got most of my things. We also went to Acme Corp, where I got the lotions, some perfumes, etc. We went to a restaurant after that, and the worst thing happened. We entered the restaurant, Central Café Park. We had one of the best tables, with an awesome view and comfy seats. Then, some girls sat down right beside our seats; we didn't really mind because it wasn't our business. So we went to wash our hands while our drinks came, and while we were going, we saw none other than Sue and her friends. Oh no... "At least they don't sit anywhere near us," Maeve whispered. We started to walk back to our table; then we thought Sue and her friends, Bea and Lula, were following us. We sat down, thinking nothing could go wrong, and then there they were, sitting right IN FRONT OF US! Maeve and I's drinks had arrived, and we also started talking about the tests we had. We were talking about how easy it would be but how nervous we still were. Then Maeve stopped mid-sentence. She neared her ears to her cushion and whispered, "I heard the word cheat; they are cheating on the test!" Woah, it's just the 4th week of school, and they are deep into cheating; I wouldn't even do that! That's hilarious; there is no way they can't be caught. Our teachers have hawk eyes. No way, we were probably going to get a bad grade on our project if we worked with Sue and Ava. So we just decided to ask to work separately; that wouldn't be a problem, we should let them know. So Maeve went over to Sue's table and said, "Since me and Lianna can't stand working with you and Ava, we are going to ask to work separately, deal?" Sue disgustedly spat out, "No, I need a good grade, and with your brains, that's all we are getting!" Thanks, Maeve. Wait, what was my first thought? Then, behind her back, she whips out her phone and plays the recording. Blackmail! What a good deal! Sue turned red with rage and embarrassment, and her food order had just arrived; it got set down 5 minutes until...

9
Disaster Struck (Maeve POV)

The food arrived right at her table. Sue, steaming with rage, went back to the table and smashed it in my face! She had some guts to do that! Lianna was helping me clean up, and Lianna took a glass of ice-cold water, added ketchup, and poured the whole glass on her. Woah, this was about to turn into a big food fight, But luckily just as Lula was about to slap more food into our faces, Lianna's hand stopped her. She said, "I don't know what your problem is, but you need to stop. You've wasted half your food by trying to throw it on us, and it barely came onto us." At that moment, Sue's mom walked in. She greeted Maeve and me, asking us what had happened. We told her all about it. Five minutes later, Sue's mom was yelling at them. Bea, Lula, and Sue looked very embarrassed. What a good day, not the best but good. They paid and left the restaurant, then when we finished eating, we paid and left. Hours later, it was 7 p.m., which was pretty late! I called my mom, asking who was picking us up; apparently, Lianna's older brother, Dylan, was picking us up. Dylan and Lianna looked like twins with brown hair, blue eyes, light freckles, and similar personalities. My mom called on the drive back, saying that she had to go on a last-minute business trip. I could stay over with Lianna! We arrived home at 7:30. We laid out our stuff and started talking. We looked and talked about our stuff and about our day. We went to the closet to put everything back, and we lay on her bed, exhausted. Let's watch a movie, I suggested. Yes! she almost yelled. Then Lianna's twin brother suddenly barged in. He looked at Lianna. He then annoyed us, "Mom said my friend can stay over too." Okay so? Lianna replied. We wanna watch movies with you guys. He replied. We reluctantly agreed; we got the snacks and got the movie ready while Lianna's twin brother, Felix, and his friend, Mark, got the couch set up with blankets, and somehow, they also got the electric fireplace going. The crazy thing is, this was all in Lianna's room. Lianna's room was the biggest except for the master bedroom, but it also had a big hidden hallway thing! We use that for other stuff. The snacks and cotton candy machine are ready, they exclaimed. We all chose a comfy spot and started to watch the movie. It was around ten now, and tomorrow was a school day, so in 10 minutes, we cleaned up and went to sleep.

10

Fun Time (Maeve POV)

---·♡·---

Lianna and I woke up early to start breakfast. She curled her medium-long hair and wore her contacts. She put on a necklace, some earrings, and some hand accessories. I already had all my stuff. Lianna wore a mushroom-patterned cardigan with a v-neck and some lazy light blonde sweatpants. I wore some ripped jeans and a light blue collar keyhole sweater. Lianna was all about style, unlike me. We raced downstairs and loaded ourselves with food. Lianna's parents were wealthy; they both had very high-paying jobs. Together, they almost made 3-4 million a year. My mom and dad both have decent jobs. Not many people know that Lianna is very wealthy. "We should dye our hair," Lianna states. "Why?" It's gonna look cool, is what she replied. Felix comes down. Felix dyes his hair a lot; he has naturally brown hair and blue eyes, but he kept his black for some time now. Lianna doesn't dye her hair as much. They were all about fashion, looks, grades, and personality. We arrived at school unprepared. "I don't wanna go in," I say. The devil might eat us out. Sue is bad, but when you're on her bad side, it's nothing good.

We actually survived the day with Sue bothering us. We arrived at P.E. with Felix and Sue. Sue is such a weirdo near Felix; she acts nice and tries to show off. It's so clear she likes him. Felix, Lianna, Mark, me, and I arrive home exhausted. Then there was a big surprise, not just one but more waiting for us. Lianna's mom, Mrs. Waylow, looked at us smiling. "Hi guys, Lianna, this is Sue and Sue, this is Lianna and Maeve." "Hold up!" Lianna began, "That girl smashed her food all over us and bullied us for the past few weeks. There is no and NO way we will let her be with us." Lianna took my hand and said, "Mimi, let's go." We ran into Felix's room and told him what had happened. He and Mark decided it would be best if we went to the park. We went through the secret hallway and took the scooters. As we were strolling through the park and talking, Felix came up with the worst possible idea. "What if Sue and her aunt make their way into mom's mind, and we are forced—" "No, that can't happen, right?" Lianna and Felix were probably devastated. People always think it's not that bad, but over the few weeks, being on Sue's bad side has been horrible. Half of the grade looks at us with disgust. Why? We don't even know, but we see Sue talking and spreading rumors. Most likely, something would happen at home. Sue could break Lianna and Felix's relationship with their mom. Mark and I saw how unhappy they looked and tried to comfort them.

"Hey, an ice cream truck!" Mark shouted, "Got any cash? It's fine if you don't, though." "I have $15 dollars in my pocket," Felix replied. "I have 10 dollars," Lianna continued. "That's more than enough," I say. We all get ice cream and head back home. As we enter the house, Mrs. Waylow stands there, hands crossed. She doesn't seem upset, but Sue is with her. She asks us why we couldn't take Sue. Felix just gets mad, and so does Lianna. We follow them upstairs where we go into Lianna's room. "She is an actual witch," I say aggravated. Lianna just collapses into her bed, and we decide to stay in the same room since it's best. Mark and I put on some music, and the atmosphere immediately changes. We dance while putting the couches together. We also put the underlying bed outside. "This is great!" we scream. We hear a knock; it's Mrs. Waylow. She starts by lecturing us and saying we should include her. I really don't like her, but I don't want to seem rude. We were going to bake cookies, so we just let Lianna and Felix do the talking, and then we went into their other kitchen where Sue won't be there. "LET'S MAKE CHRISTMAS COOKIES!" Lianna yells excitedly. "With some Christmas music," I say giggling. After an hour, we are in Felix's and Lianna's conjoined room, talking and laughing while eating cookies and milk. Then Sue comes; she doesn't knock, she barges in.

11
Problematic Problems (Lianna's POV)

Fuming red with anger, she cries out, "When can I be involved?" Felix, who is also pretty red with anger, yells, "When can you stop being a rude jerk?" She stops and leaves when her aunt and dad call her down to go. My dad doesn't arrive soon after they leave; he glances at his phone, then at mom, then back at us, and he gives us all a tired, pitiful smile. Mom comes to us and whispers, we need to have a family meeting now. I go into the room and tell Maeve and Mark we will be occupied for the next 2 hours or so. I go back down and take a seat. My mom and dad look at each other, reluctant to speak first; my dad gets to start first, "Lianna, Felix, me and your mom..." He pauses and glances at mom. Mom continues his sentence, "...are planning to get a divorce." "You can't, though!" I sputter out. My dad then starts, "This is a peaceful divorce; you will be switching from each house each week, and you guys decide if you want to switch together or not. This process may take 1-2 months.

On the last day, we decide if we are getting a divorce. If so, then you guys make the decision, together or not, and the switching begins." Mom looks and shares the same look as dad; guilt spreads over their face. Mom looks down; she frowns and looks at me, then at Felix. "I am so sorry; I know Sue and you both don't get along, but me and her dad might think of getting married after the divorce is complete. Your dad is going to be with Sue's mom, and if we do not go through the process, we will not end up as Sue's parents. I know Sue has been really mean to you, and I don't expect you to get along with her." After this announcement was made, we sat there stunned, "Sue!" Felix shouts, "Now I am done!" he mutters. I leave with Felix; we go up to the room to see Maeve and Mark laughing and talking; their happiness upsets me even more. Felix looks at me; we both are on the verge of tears by now. Sue, sister, divorce- these words were just tangled in my life now. I wanted it gone, and I had 10-11 years of happiness and memories about to be thrown away by Sue. Maeve sees our glossy eyes and comes to us, hugging us. Mark leaps at us to ask us what's wrong. Maeve looks worried and opens the window; she ties the rope in the closet with strong knots and lets it down. I see the brown cloth skimming over the brilliant, white surface. Mimi's voice shook me out of my fantasies. We can talk about it with some food, she says. She grabs her wallet, and we skim down the rope, bruising and burning our hands; we walk to the nearest food court, which quite frankly isn't that far. Suddenly, Felix's phone rings; it's Dylan; we pick up, frightened. He just asked us where we were, and he met us there. We got a lot of food, and Dylan started to talk first. "Do they know?" He looks at Mimi and

Mark. I just nod. It's new for me, too.." He says sadly. 'But at least you get to go in 2-3 years." I mumble. Dylan looks at me and says, "This isn't final."

12

"It could be!" I yell. "This is new for you guys, so I can see why you're mad. I don't want this happening either, y'know." Felix looks at Mark and says, "How was it like when your parents got divorced?" Mark sighed and said, "A part of me wants to say it wasn't that bad, but you also have to know that you don't have one home to live in. You always have to pack and then go to a new house, and when it's not peaceful, they look mad at each other with rage. They always yell at each other, and it just makes you feel bad." I decided to tell them how I felt. "It's not only the divorce, it's also about Sue. I don't want her to be with me and Felix; she is going to do something." Now Maeve was speaking, "Sue has been through her mom and dad divorcing other people too, so she is also really devastated, or she is out to get you, unbothered. This isn't new for her." I was shocked, and so was Felix. We never knew that. "Speak of the devil," Mark exclaims, and there she was, Sue, smiling and happy with her parents!

"Sue with her parents!" Maeve almost shrieked. "Shhh," I shushed her. "I know it's wrong, but I find it suspicious that she is with her parents all happy; everything seems fine! I'm gonna eavesdrop." I whisper. "So am I!" Felix almost shouted. Dylan looked at us like we were psychopaths. "So your plan of sneaking up on them is just to wear what you're wearing?" I look down. "I guess…" I mutter. "Oh no, we aren't," Felix says excitedly. "I have 2 hoodies with me, and I am wearing one right now!" He exclaims. He passes one to Mark and Maeve. "And I can give you mine." Dylan shoves his bright green hoodie toward me. "Ok, let's go," I mutter. I get my phone out to record anything valuable. As we get closer, I see them talking like a family that hasn't been divorced. I gulp. My brown hair covers my face almost fully. We sit down right next to them and start to pretend we are on our phones. Maeve and Mark on one side of them and me and Felix on the other. I take out my phone, ready to record, and I start it. I put it as near to them as I could. After they got up and left, Mark, Maeve, and Dylan came over to us. "So?" I didn't hear anything, but I'm pretty sure the recording had something," Felix says in thought. "Wait, Dylan, have they met you yet?" He just shakes his head. "No, I was in getting some stuff done. Why?"

"Perfect! Pretend like you are an integrator for a show, and you want them to be in your show, so you have to, like, give them a call and whatnot!" Dylan nods his head in agreement. "I agree, but on one condition: you HAVE to get everything we need in 2-3 weeks before I meet them." I nod my head. They started to walk, and Felix and I shooed the rest of them away. I got on my phone and started to record. The family sat down right next to us, and Dylan walked over. "Hi, I am Daniel, and I am part of a show company. We would like you to be in our show because you guys seem like a loving family. Do you agree?" Sue's dad looked at them both and nodded his head. "So, I just have to record everything you say while asking you some questions. Answers are required." Dylan looks at all of us and pretends that he doesn't know us. "Excuse me, will you guys move somewhere else?" We all nodded. Before going, I stopped and pretended to pick something up but put my phone there, just in case. What I heard, I couldn't comprehend. I didn't know what my reaction should have been.

13

Dylan: So, are you guys divorced or anything? Be honest, please. It is fine if you are divorced; we can still put you on the TV show.

Sue's Dad: No, we are not divorced. We are one loving family. *chuckles*

Dylan: Do you have any hobbies?

Sue's Mom: We try to do whatever we can, so not really.

Dylan: Any rivalries or enemies?

Sue: No, not really. But there was a time when this family thought we were divorced, so one of them would date one of my parents, and the other would date the other. But we were sort of using them for their money.

Dylan: Interesting. I will take your guys' number, and that's all!

After Dylan took Sue's dad's number, I took my phone and left. They said this was a while ago, but they could be doing this to my parents, too. I couldn't believe it! My parents might be getting used. I mean, just last week, they got promotions, so separately, they make 1-2 million. Oh no, oh no, is all I could think about. Felix tried to comfort me, but what was the use? Should we tell our parents? I spoke out, breaking the vivid, tense silence. Maeve looked so bad and sad, and Mark shared the same look. Me, Dylan, and Felix were probably on the verge of tears. I wanted to break down, but I kept it in. Dylan was so stiffened. "I'm really sorry, you guys," is all he said. We all drove silently, not wanting to face the truth, and in 1-2 weeks, Maeve had to go, and we see Sue more often.

I hated this tension, everything. Sue was a huge bully. Why did they agree to this? Were my parents out to get their children? I hated this. I just wanted to watch a movie or do something to get my mind off this. Suddenly, I spoke out, "We're telling them NOW." When we all went home, Maeve and Mark basically dove into our room while Dylan and Felix looked at our parents. Then we decided to spill what we found out.

14

I barged through the front door with Felix following me and Dylan right behind. I saw mom and dad, with a man—dressed very formally—and he was holding a couple of papers. He was sitting on our couch in front of mom and dad. A couple of drinks were in the middle of them, and the man's brown but shiny briefcase stood there. Mom looked at us, shocked, but not in a bad way, more of a pleasant way. She motioned us to sit down while dad and the random man were talking.

As they finished, mom spoke to us, "Honey, this is our lawyer, Mr. Freeman." We were shocked. Dylan sputtered out, "You said we wouldn't bring Mr. Freeman till one or two weeks." Me and Felix quite abruptly turned our heads. "YOU KNEW ABOUT THIS?" we shouted at him. "I mean, yeah, I guess," he mumbled, guilty of what he had said.

"Stop," I declare. "What do you mean by stop?" Dad asks me with the most confused look on his face. "I mean, stop with the divorce," I say louder.

Mom: Why?

Felix: Because Sue's parents aren't who you think you are.

Me: They are using you like they did for a family before!

Mom looks at Dylan and asks him if he knows about this.

Dylan: Mom, dad, I usually wouldn't agree with what they are saying, but it's true. What they are saying is true, and we have proof.

Mom: Show me then.

Dylan takes out his phone, and clicking and tapping is all I hear. Click-Tap-Click-Tap. He looks at us, then mom and dad. "It's gone! I must have deleted it by accident." I was suddenly mad and sad, but I remember I had it on my phone! I pull out my phone and play the recording. Mom and Dad look at us like we are gods or something. They have a flood of emotions, and all I can see is them and their glossy eyes. They tell Mr. Freeman that they wouldn't like to go through the divorce, and then they look at us, and I look at Dylan, expecting him to be happy, but he has glossy eyes, too. "What happened, Dylan?" Felix asks.

15

He stands there looking down, "I'm sorry," he whispers. "For what?" Felix asks him. He looks at all of us again. "I just can't tell you now, but if you find out, please don't be mad at me." He walked away and out the door. I heard his car engine, but it still lingered in my mind. What did he mean by that? The whole night I tossed and turned; it lingered in my head. I was going to burst! Then I woke up the next day not expecting weird things to happen. I wake up at 4 AM, thinking it's 7 AM and get ready. I chose the best possible outfit I could. Just my luck, Dylan is dropping me. We get into the car, and the entire 5 minutes are silent. When we finally arrived at the parking lot at school, I dashed as fast as a cheetah outside and caught up with Maeve. When I finally caught up with her, we sauntered toward the building to see Felix and Mark. Mark and Felix looked bored and looked like they were dying of boredom, but then I saw them fiddling with their phones together. We walk into the school rather early and slump right next to our lockers. We sneak out our phones and start to play games and watch TikTok and YouTube. Maeve thinks of the idea of walking around school, so we open our lockers. Bella's was on the top while mine was on the bottom, while Maeve shoves her backpack into her locker. I carefully place it on the hanger in my locker.

Maeve slams her locker shut and bends down right next to me.

"Lollipop?" She asks me.

I reluctantly reach into the farthest part of my locker and pull out a lollipop. She squeals as she takes the lollipop. I quickly pull out a cookie from my locker and start to munch on it while we walk around school. We know it isn't right to eat sugary things in the morning, but how could we help it? My locker had junk food. The lockers in school were surprisingly big enough for all of that.

As we saunter around school, we come across a sign that reads in big letters:

!HONOR ROLLS TODAY!

Maeve stares at the sign, hoping she would get an honor roll, and I was hoping I would get one, too. I put my hand on her shoulder and led her the other way. We bump into the choir hall to hear high-pitched singing, which soon stops for some reason. I turn my head around and see them handing out doughnuts.

"Ew," she sneers quietly. "What time is it?"

"Oh, 8:03, let's head back," I whisper back.

But then I saw our friend Alli, and I couldn't stop but start waving vigorously at her. She stares back at me and waves back, mouthing she will be at my locker. We happily saunter to our locker to see her already standing there looking at me. I groan as I unlock my locker and give her a piece of Reese's.

"I'm thirsty," I say.

"Back to the cafeteria!" We yell as we dash through the hall.

As we get into the cafeteria, we see only a handful of kids eating breakfast there. We stop to get water, Coke, etc., and a few cinnamon rolls. I give Alli, Maeve, and myself a Coke and stuff the rest in my locker. We go back to our lockers where we just continue to be on our phones, and as the bell rings, we head to our classes.

16

Maeve and I face our lockers, impatiently waiting for the bell to ring so we can dig through them. As soon as we hear the bell ring, we start digging into our lockers. I have no idea what Maeve was doing, but she got her Spanish book out first, which was surprising because I already had my books out. I was putting my lunch box away when I noticed her eating another lollipop. I took my Spanish book out carefully and held it against my chest with my hands wrapped around the book. I quietly sneak behind her.

"BOO!" I yell while laughing.

She turns around, facing me with THREE lollipops in her mouth.

"Not funny," she mumbles. "Let's match!"

She hands me three lollipops, and I shove them into my mouth, and the sourness soaks my mouth. We walk into class with our Spanish teacher looking at us.

"Candy? Already?" He questions sarcastically.

"Oh, of course!" Maeve spits out.

That candy must be giving her more confidence than usual. We sit at our table, where there are four people: me, Felix, Maeve, and Felix's other friend, Will. His name is William, but everyone calls him Will. The tables can seat around six people, so our table is usually "empty." As Maeve and I start to finish our Spanish warm-up, we start talking off-topic with Felix and Will. Our Spanish teacher and the rest of our class started to shush us. Mr. Holmes, our Spanish teacher, tells us that two new people have got a schedule change and are in this class. He introduced Shay, who I already knew since he was part of my brother's group of friends. He smirks at me, and I roll my eyes. There was one person I hated more than Sue, Shay. Shay sits at our table, which is not that surprising. And remember Sue? Oh yeah, she is also a new student. I eye her so hard I think my eyeball would pop out. She sits down right next to Shay, who is right next to me and starts to act all innocent. I hated every single gut of her. Maeve starts to make jokes, and while we giggle together, she side-eyes me, and I roll my eyes back; two can play that game.

"You have the brain size of a rat!" She insults me. The comment is not supposed to hurt, but I feel a sharp pain every time she insults me.

"Little Miss Rich isn't used to insults, I guess," she taunts.

I couldn't take it anymore, so I ran out of the classroom. I was able to collapse in a bathroom stall. I took out my phone with my hands shaking and dialed my mom, and when she didn't pick up, all I could do was burst into more quiet sobs. I could hear someone running in the halls, and I couldn't care less until I heard my brother's voice.

"Lianna?" He called out into the bathroom. "Lianna?"

I came out, and he embraced me into a hug. Not those hugs where you're forced to hug for a picture, this hug felt genuine, and I just sobbed to him. I feel Maeve hugging me, too, and then Will and Shay, and I smiled. I smiled, knowing that I have people who care about me.

"We should get to class," I mumbled.

"I think so too," Maeve replied.

We enter class to see everyone doing work. They all look at me and then Sue. Sue sees me, and her eyes soften, not too much, but I see it. I ignore her presence, and so does everyone else.

After some time, Mr. Holmes calls me out into the hall.

"Lianna, I want to know if you're okay," he asks me concerningly.

"I'm good," I reply dryly. He always favors Sue because she has a typical look: blonde hair, and blue eyes. He would take Sue's side on this, too. "May I go back in now?" I say, slightly annoyed.

He sighs. "Yes, you may."

After some time, 1ˢᵗ period was over, and I couldn't be happier, but then I had art. Since Will and Shay got a schedule change, they were in all my classes. So all my close friends were in all of my classes. We all went to art but stopped by Felix's locker (which was right next to mine) so we could get some drinks from his mini-fridge. During 2nd period, Maeve and I needed to go to the bathroom, so we went. As we approached the bathroom, we heard sobs. It wasn't our problem. I mean, it was probably some 7th or 8th grader crying because their boyfriend or girlfriend broke up with them. However, I soon realized I knew that voice.

"Lianna, Maeve, DON'T GO THERE!" a voice shouted.

Suddenly, everything went black.

17

I woke up with a pain in my back and looked down to see blood. Not too much, but it was enough to make me pass out again.

"Are you okay?" I see another one of Felix's friends hovering over me.

"I'm good," I say, trying to lift myself up, but I fail miserably.

"Why is my back hurting so much, and where is Maeve?"

"I can answer both," he says proudly. "As soon as I yelled at you not to go in there, you entered, and where you ended up, there were a couple of pins on the bathroom floor I could visibly see from here. Maeve fell too, but instead of being unconscious and stabbed by pins, she was fine, and she is calling your brother right now."

"That's a lot of information," I manage to sputter out.

"Yeah, that is," Milo replies.

I try to lay back down comfortably, but as soon as I close my eyes, nausea sets in.

"Lianna," I hear multiple yells.

I see Felix shocked, and he bends over.

"That must be painful," Will speaks for him.

Maeve shouts, "Don't you guys have ANY common sense? Let's call the nurse instead of "ooing over blood."

I smile, and Milo and Maeve run off to the nurse. I lay my head on Felix's hand.

He looks down at me with sadness. Then I hear tap-tap-tap, the sound of heels making contact with the floor. Soon, the nurse is towering over me, inspecting the blood all over me. I lay down on a stretcher while they call 911. I then remember them plucking out the needles, which was very painful, and then getting a back brace, which limits a lot of things we can do in everyday life.

I miss a lot of periods, but I do convince my reluctant doctor and parents that I can attend the 6th through 8th period. I would call them if I needed anything. I enter 6th-period science, and as I walk into class, everyone's eyes are on me. Sue tries to smile at me, but I ignore her. My science teacher, my favorite teacher, looks down at me and lets me skip some activities if I wanted to. However, overall school was alright, but I couldn't wait to see Dylan's reaction.

As the day flew by, I was at home with Felix and our group of friends, I guess. Which is Axel, Ray, Miles, Milo, Lucas, Landon, Will, Shay, Jace, Jonah, and Maeve. Maeve and I prefer to be known as off to the side. When we got home toward Felix's and my room, I could only limp and wince in pain the entire way up the stairs. I couldn't use the elevator because it was undergoing some small but significant renovations. We all just lay on the couch, talking, playing, and eating. Then Will came up with the most brilliant idea: a game of hide and seek. Playing the game was the most fun, even though Will was my partner. I loved playing. We really made an awesome team. Suddenly, the front door opened, and we turned to see what was going on. I only sobbed more.

18

It not only affected me but also Felix. Walking through the door were Dylan and Sue, smiling and laughing together. As soon as Dylan saw mine and Felix's faces, he ran up the stairs, but we walked quickly enough to slam the door in his face. He kept knocking and knocking, but Felix and I were too stubborn. At one point, we had to get dinner, so we ordered it because Felix was fixed on not eating anything Dylan made. As the bell rang, I offered to go and get the food, and so did Jace, so we went together while laughing about the TikToks we found. I honestly just wanted to let my legs get some exercise. As we turned around, I saw Dylan with a shocked expression. I looked down. Oh, he was looking at my brace.

"What happened?" He asked, sounding concerned.

"Why do you care?" I asked dryly.

I walked as carefully as I could up the stairs, and when I saw how flabbergasted he was, I just smiled. You might think I took it too far, but siding with my archenemy, no way. We heard a knock on the door; we knew who it was, Dylan. Dylan looked guilty as he handed me a box.

"This is a present for you and Felix," He said, looking down.

I took it and nodded my head slowly, closing the door in his face.

"Ooh, a present!" Felix squealed.

He swiftly grabbed it from my hand and opened it, and he looked disappointed.

"What's in there?" I asked, concerned.

He groaned. "You might like this."

He shoved the half-opened box into my hands, and then I saw paper, long strips of paper. Not multiple, probably like thirty papers.

"THIS IS CHAE YEONG'S CONCERT TICKETS!" I yelled.

"I know," Felix grumbled.

"There are fifteen tickets, so everyone can go with us," I spoke excitedly.

"Boring," all the boys yelled.

"I think we should go; there's gonna be a lot of food there," I tempted them.

"Deal!" Landon said.

"Wait, you said there are fifteen tickets?" He questioned.

"Yeah," I said, suspicious of what he was going to say.

"There looks like there are like fifty pieces in there," he stated.

We emptied out the entire box to find plane tickets to none other than Europe! As I looked closer, I saw that it was France!

Everyone cheered except me; we had three extra tickets. Who do we use them on?

"I mean, Dylan did pay for the tickets," Tristan says.

"So?" I ask.

"Maybe we should let him come," he replies.

"I think not," Felix answers. "He backstabbed us, no more explanation and no more talking about it."

Right at that moment, someone knocks on the door. I open it to see Sue. I don't even let her talk. I slam the door in her face. She knocks again, "Can we talk?"

"Fine, make it snappy."

I let her in; she looked at the ticket and breathed.

"I really am sorry. I just hated how you would embarrass me. You're wealthy, and my entire family wanted to attack your family," she said.

I stopped; that was kind. She smiled devilishly at me. "Could I come to the concert too?"

Felix steps in. "So that's what it's about, the concert?"

"You're messed up," I told her.

She ran out of the room crying. Hopefully, she was gone.

A knock again, Felix opened the door. "Literally stop, Sue."

Dylan stands there looking mad. "So what she said is true?" he questioned. "You did make Sue cry and say bad things about her? I can't believe I ever gave you that gift, and Lianna, you deserve that brace."

I looked at him, shocked. "You took it too far, and if that's what you think, take the gift, but you will not hurt me or Lianna or anyone in this room. Even better, don't talk to us."

Dylan was mixed with emotions; I limped my way over to the door and shoved it as hard as I could. I lay as comfortably as I could on the bed with my broken back and broken heart.

The next day at school, there was a new student from Singapore. I thought she was okay and cool. Maeve and I eventually started talking to her, and our group became a trio. Even though it was a little obvious, they both were closer to me than they both were to each other. At one point, Peggy and Maeve became inseparable too; it was the happiest trio ever.

As time went on, we saw how rude Peggy was to people, and how she gossiped too much. I said nothing, but Maeve had a problem with it, I think.

"Lianna, do you notice that Peggy is being self-absorbed? I don't mean to be that type of person who gossips, but who am I? She keeps judging everyone and hating them. We should back out of the friendship before it becomes too toxic," she whispered.

"For once, I agree with you. Let's do it then," I agreed.

From then on, we kept our distance from Peggy, but it was a bit hard too, since she had lunch and three other classes with us. She might have noticed because she came up to us and asked why we were avoiding her. I told her we were just busy, but from then on, it was like we were walking on eggshells.

At one point, Maeve came up with a quick excuse and took my hand to run away. She pulled me to a corner and said, "We have to end things before anything goes seriously wrong," Mimi said.

I nodded reluctantly, even though I had lots of friends, I had never done this.

"So, who is going to, like, tell her first?" I asked.

"It depends, probably not you, because she was really close to you," she answered.

I was happy it wasn't me breaking the news to her, but I still knew I had to back up Mimi.

19

During the passing period when we saw Peggy, we approached her.

"Oh hey guys! Do you guys like my Lululemon skirt? Does it match with my Vineyard Vines shirt? My mom is taking me shopping for..." Mim interrupted Peggy.

"Listen, Peggy. We used to love being your friend, but now I think you are being a bit self-observant, and this friendship is getting pretty toxic."

"Me? Toxic?" She scoffed.

I had to back up Maeve. "Like just now? You didn't ask how our day was or what we were gonna do. Listen, Peggy, you have been this self-observant girl for the past few weeks, and you don't care about us. You gossip too much, and whenever we get into a fight, you are always the victim." I stopped myself. Maeve looked at me, and we both walked away without another word.

We stopped at my locker to get some snacks and on the way to World Cultures, where we would have to see her again. As we entered the room, Peggy wasn't there, so I happily shuffled toward my spot. Then Sue and Peggy walked in together. When they saw me and Maeve, they side-eyed us, and I couldn't blame Peggy. Felix walked up to me.

"Since when did they become friends?"

"Ever since this morning," I told him.

"Well, I got 9 tickets for Chae Yeong's concert."

"No way!" I said, flabbergasted.

"It's in 2 weeks, so invite some people that you want."

I nodded in agreement.

"Hey, what happened, why so excited?" Maeve asked me.

"Mim... will you go to Chae Yeong's concert with me?" I asked excitedly.

"Yes! A thousand times, yes!" She answered.

20

After 2 weeks, we were getting ready to go. It was me, Felix, Maeve, Jonah, Shay, Jaden, Jenny, Levi, and Lucas.

I was beyond excited, and Felix, Maeve, and I got VIP tickets. I couldn't wait more than to meet her in person! The concert was 4 hours, and the BEST 4 hours of my life. I screamed so loud I couldn't even whisper. When we all met her backstage, she was so nice, and I hugged her so tight I bet she choked. We got really friendly, and soon I was talking to her about my life problems. The advice she gave me changed my life. I told her about how it was hard for me to speak freely, and I hated being judged for not being able to speak the right words.

"You're doing it right now! No matter who judges you, you never let them get to you because who you are should never change. Try. Try to speak to people, try to let them get to know you," Chae Yeong told me.

She told me of her fears and how they may have traumatized herself too. Tonight was the best night of my life. I learned so many things about her, and I just loved her company. I realized that Chae Yeong got hate that she never should have got. I realized that some people are shallow, and they judge so much. Chae Yeong fought everything; she fought death threats and hate notes. She told me how some of her friends, who were K-pop idols, wanted to commit suicide because of this cyberbullying. K-Pop idols can be seen as jokes, and people don't realize the damage they do to them. I loved that night, and I cherish it so much!

Felix and Maeve really got to know her, too. The one thing she said to me changed my life.

"Some people look for a beautiful place. Others make a place beautiful."

21

(Chae Yeong)

—♭—

I felt on top of the moon when I was performing my show; never did I know that was going to be my last one. That show might have been my favorite; the crowd sang with me. It's like everyone there knew me, not the famous me but the personality inside me. I met three brilliant kids at the VIP lounge. They were intimidating at first; they looked sophisticated, but it's like they knew me. They were so similar to me in terms of their daily life problems.

One girl, Lianna, really stood out to me; she was funny and almost looked like me. She talked about how I've always been her idol and how easy I've made it look to be an idol. I told her about my life and how it was the opposite of easy. They all had some problems in their life, and I was pretty happy I found someone to relate to. I told them about my life and my childhood. Two weeks later, I was about to start my next show, but with all the yelling and the pressure on me, I just couldn't handle it, I guess.

22

(Lianna)

I was in awe that I got to meet my idol, but it all came crashing down two weeks later. Felix ran up to me, and he looked worried; behind him was Dylan, and he seemed worried, too. Felix shoved the phone in my face, and there was a picture of Chae Yeong. I heard Isabella gasp behind me. It wasn't any picture. It looked like she was in a janitor's closet, and there was a rope that was attached to her neck. She hung herself; she committed suicide, and I knew why. I told her about the pressure I went through, but I never knew the pressure she took would result in this. I felt like I lost a family member. I heard Sue giggling behind the door, and for once I had enough. I slammed the door smack in her face. Dylan went outside, and seconds later I heard him yelling. I was scared; it was like my world was collapsing right at my feet, and there was nothing I could do about it. She made such a huge impact. In reality, the K-pop industry was filled with different emotions, and K-pop idols would do anything to keep their family and fans happy and safe. Every idol feels like they have been stabbed in the gut with all the hate they get, but we would never know. Idols deserve the world; they don't get to be treated like a punching bag. Chae Yeong was like a soldier who lost their battle through pressure. Right now, I am thinking of all the bad memories, but what about the happy ones? I think about her relationship with other idols. She was a pretty and smart girl. She was a great vocalist, and she stood proud on stage. He showed how happy she was, but inside, she felt like nothing. I haven't lost Chae Yeong; she just gained her wings earlier than other idols.

People join the K-pop community only to make fun of it and mistreat, rumor, and hurt idols just to be "funny". Later, maybe in a few weeks, months, or years, this is what would happen to them: everyone crying around them. Idols are humans, and humans have feelings; they weren't born to be punching bags. Idols may be doing something racist, homophobic, or even mistreating shouldn't tell them to kill themselves.

www.ingramcontent.com/pod-product-compliance
Lightning Source LLC
Chambersburg PA
CBHW021754150726
47989CB00004B/1654